About the Author

I am Adeoba Debayo-Doherty. This is my second book. I am thirty-one years of age. I am studious and quiet, and I just love writing books.

A Spy and a Terror

Adeoba Debayo-Doherty

A Spy and a Terror

Olympia Publishers
London

www.olympiapublishers.com
OLYMPIA PAPERBACK EDITION

A CIP catalogue record for this title is
available from the British Library.

ISBN: 978-1-80074-511-7

This is a work of fiction.
Names, characters, places and incidents originate from the writer's
imagination. Any resemblance to actual persons, living or dead, is
purely coincidental.

First Published in 2022

Olympia Publishers
Tallis House
2 Tallis Street
London
EC4Y 0AB

Printed in Great Britain

Dedication

I'd like to dedicate this book to everyone who has ever loved.

Acknowledgements

I'd like to thank Olympia publishers for the publication of this book.

CHAPTER ONE

It's Kingfisher Jack's third year at Cambridge University and he's got to get no less than an A plus in physics to get into Oxford for his fourth year. Countdown a hundred and thirty days.

Day 1: Eight cups of water every hour. One too many, that will do. Shows he's nervous.

Day 2: Goes out on a date with his girlfriend and pops the question.

Day 3: Buys a large size paper sheet and a clip board.

Day 4: Draws out an extensive plan detailing every aspect of his university life to work life.

Day 5: He studies fifty-four chapters on quantum mechanics, and is so sleepy he shuts his eyes and sleeps for sixteen hours.

Day 6: He studies astronomy in physics

Day 7: Takes his fiancée out for some pizza

Day 8: Takes his dog out for a walk. Oops. Smelly poop.

Day 9: He studies the black red hole.

Day 10: He studies *The Autobiography Of Einstein, His World and His Universe.*

Day 11: He studies speed, mass and time…

… … …

Day 69: Kingfisher Jack marries and his mum and dad don't turn up.

REASON: He should have graduated from university first.

… … …

Day 128: Thorough revision of coursework.

Day 129: Recuperation. Enough rest for the big day

CHAPTER TWO

On the one hundred and sixty-sixth day counting from the first, Kingfisher gets his papers from his physics teacher. An A plus. He goes home to celebrate with his wife, Lucy Jack, nee Redmond. They also call some friends whom they've known since their freshman year over to have a cookout with some BBQ ribs, hot dogs and American beef burgers.

Kingfisher is originally African American, born and bred in Hawaii. He moved to Europe two years ago and has adjusted well to the UK life making many friends. He's also in the Afro-Caribbean society and the track team. All fun ends though, because fourth year is the hardest for engineering students.

CHAPTER THREE

The following April, a new child is born. Lisa Jack. Kingfisher is far behind on his coursework and will only manage to get a C grade if he aces the exam.

He meets up with the professor and tells him about his condition. First, the professor pauses then offers him a book. 'See, I've never read it but they say it does wonders.'

'Who's they?'

'The experts. Anyway, I've got to go.'

'Thanks, professor.'

'It's alright, Kingfisher'.

Kingfisher searches the entire book at home and he comes across chapter seventeen, "Travelling to the Future". He brings out his highlighter and highlights the necessary parts for him.

CHAPTER FOUR

Kingfisher finds in the book that you can time travel with a special kind of jump suit and whistle costing a hundred thousand dollars. He doesn't have that kind of money so he goes to borrow the money from a bank. He travels to the future and sees his exam question paper as the professor is typing. He copies everything word for word till the end. And then flies back to the present. He aces the test eventually.

CHAPTER FIVE

'Babe, where would you like to go for summer?'

'I don't know. Anywhere my sugar bunny wants.'

'OK, I tell you where we'll go.'

'Hmm, let's go to Spain. I'll book the tickets tomorrow.'

Kingfisher uses an overdraft of ten thousand dollars to gamble for a million dollars on roulette. He wears his jumpsuit and whistle, jumps to a minute later and sees where the ball lands. He writes it on a sheet of paper and travels back to the present. He wins the game and the million dollars. The first thing he does is go to the bank to repay his loan and overdraft. Then he, Lucy and Lisa go on their July treat. Somewhere along the line, Kingfisher tells Lucy how he got the money but refuses to tell her about the time travel thing. 'OK, honey, as long as you win.'

CHAPTER SIX

With this modern technology, Kingfisher graduates with all honours easily. He ends up not doing a masters and starts up an engineering firm. Five years later, he moves back to America and runs for president.

...

...

He wins!

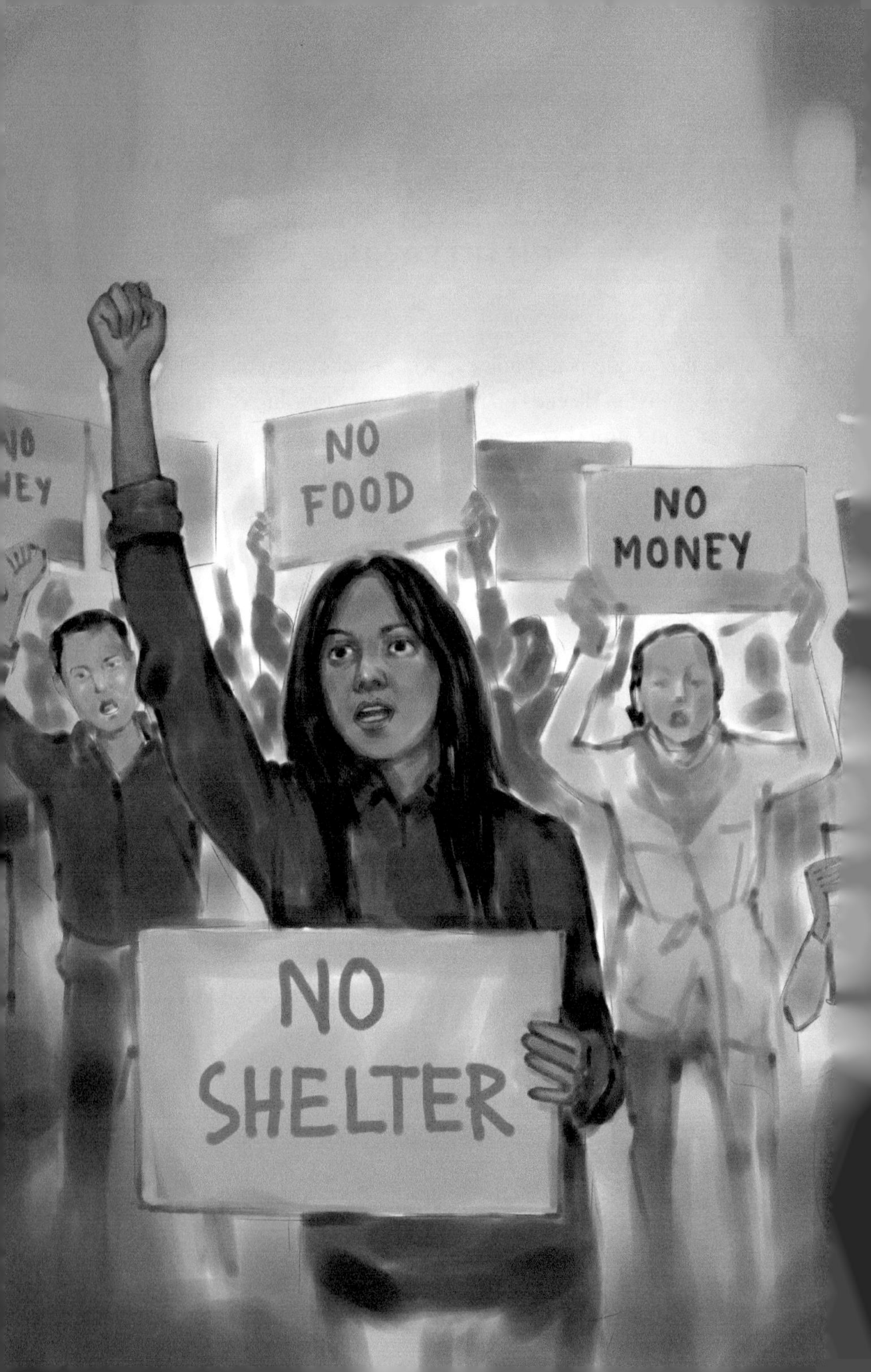
NO FOOD
NO MONEY
NO SHELTER

CHAPTER SEVEN

Little Ingham is born to Dick and Mary. Little Ingham lives in the future. She is a red Indian living in Oklahoma, America. The future is full of paradise and there is no war or bloodshed. It is unusually warm throughout the year. She would play with the other kids and come home at five to her parents, Dick and Mary. Her parents make sure she reads several books a day. She finds a book that shows one how to use a hat to go back in time. The hat costs five hundred pounds. She buys it at Alleys on Tuesday and she leaves on the same day. There are protests and riots all over America. She doesn't flee because even though the violence persists, the luxury of the environment is speck and span. She stares at a statue, beaming, until five men charge at her, nearly beating her to death, raping her. She picks up her hat and disappears back to the future, telling no one.

CHAPTER EIGHT

Dick and Mary are wondering why their daughter has been looking up karate books and books on knives.

Ingram wears her hat, tracks the exact timeline where she was raped and allocates what timeline the suspects are at. Once she finds them, she kills them with a pocket knife and heads back to the future.

CHAPTER NINE

Lisa Jack sneaks into her father's room to get some fresh lemon tea when she sees a jumpsuit and a whistle. 'Dad?! Dad!' Kingfisher and Lucy sneak out the house looking kinky.

'Go to sleep!' So Lisa takes the jumpsuit and whistle, and delves into the future.

She is shocked that everywhere is so peaceful until she sees a girl from a distance with blood all over her dress. 'Hey! Hey you!' Ingram runs. Lisa retreats.

When Lisa comes home, Mum and Dad get back. Lisa pretends to sleep and they call it a night.

CHAPTER TEN

Next morning, while Kingfisher was out, Lisa and Lucy are watching TV. There are some disturbing images – five men are found dead in Oklahoma city centre. Lisa is beginning to link the murder of those five men to the blooded dress girl she saw in the future, then she tells her mum about everything.

CHAPTER ELEVEN

Thirteen years later, Lisa, twenty-seven, becomes an investigative spy working on the case of Ingham's murder. Ingham has previously stated that she doesn't want to go to court, that she'll like to be investigated instead. Lisa walks into the room confidently.

'Hi Ingham, my name is Lisa.'

They shake hands.

'Ingham, I once saw you as a girl thirteen years ago. You were covered in blood. Why's that?' Lisa asks.

'I did it for justice'

'Well, how do you mean?'

'The men I butchered had raped me previously.'

'I know it seems odd Ingham but could you prove it?'

'Yes, if we go back in time.'

CHAPTER TWELVE

So the pair go back in time the following day, have a day's rest, and come back for further investigation.

'You do know you should have told the police and what you did was manslaughter?' said Lisa

'You might say so but I'd never heard of the police.'

'I see, but do you think what you call justice was fair to those men and their families?'

'No, but where I'm from, there is no violence and all this was new to me.'

'But your notes said you saw protestors demonstrating and you still gazed at the statues.'

'But I didn't know the men were going to rape me.'

'Which is to say you prefer riches and violence?!'

'No'

'No further questions. We'll resolve the situation in two weeks.'

As Lisa left the investigation room, she was congratulated by everyone.

CHAPTER THIRTEEN

The next morning, the case was out in the newspapers with the title "Wanna Kill Someone? Just Go Back to the Past". Lisa sat down to have coffee while her husband, Tuk, was out there cooking in the kitchen.

CHAPTER FOURTEEN

Lisa and Tuk were out in the Bahamas for holiday. They rented a condo by the ocean. They would go on the sand and talk to some of the neighbours. They celebrated their fifth wedding anniversary on the sandy shores of the Bahamas. It was splendid. They invited some of the friends that they had made. They had cakes, sweets, minced pies and wine. The couple were both knackered after.

At midnight, their house was on fire and it woke the couple up. Lisa's phone was beeping and there was a text on her phone from Ingham saying, "Me. Escaped". Lisa tries to look up the fire emergency number but there's no internet on her phone.

The building was falling into bits and there's only room for one person to exit.

'Just go!' Tuk says.

'No! I'm not going without you,' responds Lisa.

Tuk repeats, 'Just go!' and when the fire almost consumes Lisa, she makes it out. However, Tuk dies in the fire. She goes back to Oklahoma devastated. She visits her parents for comfort and restoration.

CHAPTER FIFTEEN

She returns to the F.B.I. office and the team get to work. They begin on a plan – to find Ingham and put her in prison. How they were going to do it was to get Lisa to undergo plastic surgery and form into a man, the best looking man ever. Second, the team were going to teach Lisa how to charm by personality and character ethics. Third, they were to marry and Lisa was to jot down every single thing about Ingham and she was to report it back to the team.

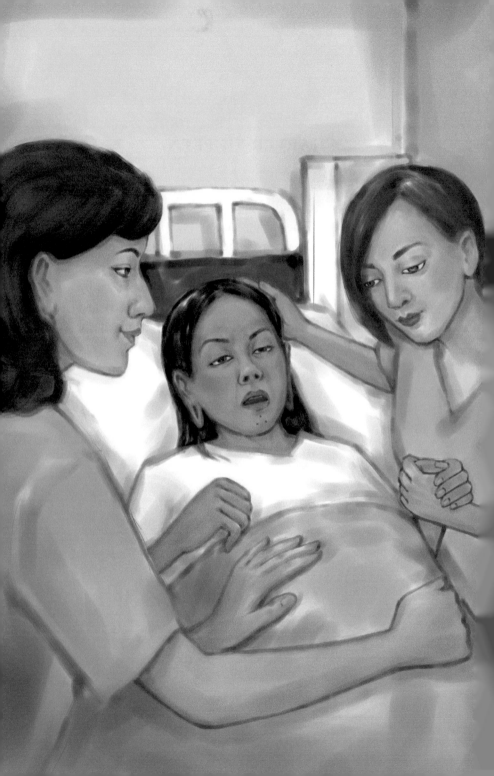

CHAPTER SIXTEEN

Two years later, they married and Lisa called herself Etingham Bolly. Etingham's real age was twenty-nine but she faked twenty-five. Ingham was also twenty-five.

Ingham wanted children so Etingham went to surgery to pass sperm. Etingham tried not to get too close to Ingham so while Ingham was not in the house, she would make copies of their photos, shred them up and burn them in the fireplace. Ingham gave birth to a boy and called him Fred. Ingham trusted Etingham with every secret and finally confided in her about her past. Etingham advised Ingham to give herself in and she finally did. Etingham changed back to Lisa and handled the case. Ingham was sentenced to life in prison in a women's confinement with no parole in a luxury prison for killing a spy's husband and endangering the lives of many Americans by killing five men.

CHAPTER SEVENTEEN

Lisa took Fred underneath her wing and their relationship blossomed over the years.